SUGAR CREEK GANG
ON THE
MEXICAN BORDER

SUGAR CREEK GANG
ON THE
MEXICAN BORDER

Original title:
Sugar Creek Gang on the Mexican Border

Paul Hutchens

MOODY PRESS • CHICAGO

Sugar Creek Gang on the Mexican Border

Copyright 1950 by
Paul Hutchens

Moody Press Edition 1968

ISBN 0-8024-4818-6

13 15 17 19 20 18 16 14

Printed in the United States of America

1

Long before we left Sugar Creek for our winter vacation along the Rio Grande River, I had been sure that when we went fishing down there we'd catch a fish as big as a boy. I was *so* sure of it, that I started in telling nearly everybody I met about it. Why, that great big fish we were going to land might even be as big as Little Jim, the smallest member of our gang, or maybe as big around as Poetry, the barrel-shaped member, the most mischievous one of us, who, because he wants to be a detective some day, is always getting us mixed up in some mysterious and exciting adventure.

But say, when instead of a big fish, we caught something else just as big and had to pounce down upon it and hold onto it for dear life or it would have gotten away—and also had to keep on holding on or we'd maybe have gotten our eyes scratched out or ourselves badly slashed up—well, I just couldn't have imagined anything so excitingly different happening to a gang of ordinary boys.

Of course our gang wasn't exactly ordinary. Anyway, Circus, our acrobat and expert wrestler, wasn't; Big Jim, our fuzzy-moustached leader, wasn't either; neither was Dragonfly, the popeyed member who was always seeing exciting things first and also was always sneezing at the wrong time because he was allergic to nearly everything. Certainly Little Jim, the smallest one of us, wasn't ordinary. He was an especially good boy which any ordinary boy knows isn't exactly ordinary. He wasn't any sissy though, as you'll see for yourself when I get to that part of the story where Little Jim joined in the struggle we were having with a very savage, wild, mad something-or-other one moonlit night on the American side of the Rio Grande.

Even I myself, Bill Collins, red-haired and freckle-faced and a little bit fiery-tempered part of the time, wasn't exactly ordinary. Anyway my mother says most of the time I don't even act like what is called "normal"—whatever that is.

Well here goes with the story of the Sugar Creek Gang along the Rio Grande. The Rio Grande is a wet boundary between Mexico and America and is a big, long, wide, reddish-brown river that the people who live down at the bottom of Texas have harnessed up and put to work for them—kind of like Dad harnesses up old Topsy, our brownish mud-colored horse, and drives her around all over the Sugar Creek territory wherever he wants to. The way they harnessed up the river was by digging miles and miles of ditches for its water to flow in all around through the Rio Grande Valley to irrigate their orange and lemon and grapefruit groves and truck patches where they grow cabbage and lettuce and carrots and other garden stuff. They also sterilize some of the water to make it safe for drinking and cooking.

Of course a lot of interesting things happened to our gang before that last exciting day—and night, especially—but I'll just sort of skim over them quick so I can get to the most dangerous part in less than maybe a couple of dozen pages. In almost less than a jiffy, I'll be galloping with you right through the—but you wait and see what.

"Maybe my daddy will buy a grapefruit grove down along the Rio Grande in Texas, and maybe we'll move down there to live," Dragonfly said to me sadly about two days before we left for the Rio Grande Valley. He had come over to my house to play with me that snowy morning, and he and I were out in the barn cracking black walnuts and gobbling up the kernels as fast as we could. I noticed that every now and then his face would get a messed-up expression on it and he would sneeze, which meant he either had a cold or was allergic to something or other in our barn.

Hearing him say that didn't make me feel very happy, 'cause even though he sometimes was sort of a nuisance to the gang, he'd been one of us as long as any of us had, and it would make a very sad hole in our gang if he left us for good.

"Daddy says we'll have to try out the climate first to see if we like it," he said, still sad in his voice and on his face. Then he added hopefully, "I hope I have to sneeze every five minutes after we get there."

"Why?" I said.

8

" 'Cause I'd rather live up here at Sugar Creek where I only have to sneeze every *seven* minutes"—which would have been funny if it hadn't been almost true.

Just that minute Mom's voice came quavering out across our cold, snowy barnyard like it does when she is calling me to come to the house for a while for something, and in only a few jiffies Dragonfly and I were both diving headfirst through the snowstorm to our back door.

Say, almost the very second we got inside our house Dragonfly started in sneezing like a house afire, and it wasn't because of the swell-smelling dinner Mom was cooking on our kitchen stove, either.

It was after we went into our living room where Mom and Charlotte Ann, my baby sister, were that Dragonfly let out those stormy sneezes, six or seven of them in fast succession. Right away he exclaimed, "I smell somebody's perfume!"

I quick looked at Mom's friendly, motherly face to see if her nose had any shine on it like it sometimes has when she's been working in the kitchen and hasn't remembered to powder it, and it was a little bit shiny, so maybe Dragonfly was mistaken, I thought.

"The doctor says I'm allergic to some kinds of face powder," Dragonfly said, screwing up his face and sneezing three more times in even quicker succession than he had the other time. He looked with worried eyes first at Mom and then at Charlotte Ann, who, I noticed, was over in the corner of the living room sitting on the floor. She had Mom's face powder box open and some of the powder had spilled out, making it look like somebody had scattered peach-colored dust over about three square feet of the rug.

Right away, Dragonfly and I were out of doors, getting there quicker than our old Mixy-cat could have gone if Dragonfly's Airedale dog had been chasing her.

All of a sudden, I got what wasn't a very bright idea. "You don't *have* to stay down south if you don't want to," I said to him.

"Why?"

"If you *can* really sneeze a lot while you're there, your folks won't move down to stay, will they?"

"No, but what if I *can't?* I can only sneeze

when I'm close to something I'm allergic to." He scooped up a double handful of snow, made a ball of it, whirled and threw it across the barnyard through the fast falling flakes toward old Topsy, who was standing on the east side of the barn, with her tail to the wind like horses do if they're outdoors standing in a storm.

"Look," I said, "let me fix you up a little box of Mom's face powder, and when you get down there, you—well you'll know what to do with it."

He looked at me with a sneezy expression on his face and said, "I couldn't fool Dad; besides my mother would smell the powder on me and wonder if I was turning into a girl or something. She might even be allergic to it herself. She says I inherited the sneezes from her."

I knew several other things Dragonfly had maybe inherited from her, such as believing it meant bad luck if a black cat crossed your path or if you broke a looking glass, and good luck if you found a horseshoe. He also had a hard time not believing in ghosts, even though he went to our church and had become an actual Christian one day when he was sliding down a sycamore tree along Sugar Creek, like Zacchaeus did in the

Bible. Because his mother believed in ghosts—or almost did anyway—it made it hard for him not to.

Dragonfly had a swell mother though, but he being her only boy, she worried about him too much, and that worried him.

Well, even my dad got what Mom called the "warm-climate bug," and because Mom hadn't had any vacation for years, we decided to take our car and drive down to the bottom of Texas, too. That meant that with two cars going there'd be room in the back seats for six boys to go along—which is how many of us there are in our gang—except Little Tom Till, the seventh one of us, who had to stay home and help take care of his mother. He also was going to help his father do the chores for us while my family was gone.

Maybe I had better explain to you right this very second before I go any farther how in the world a gang of school-age boys could get to go on a swell, warm-climate vacation in the middle of a cold winter, 'cause if I don't, nearly every mother who reads about us getting to go will wonder, "What on earth—and why?" And some of them might even start to worry about us.

Well, it just so happened that a lot of coal

miners in the United States, not even knowing how bad we all needed a vacation from school, went on what is called a "strike" and stayed on it for so long that the schools around Sugar Creek got so low on coal that most of them had to close for a while.

You could have knocked us over with a snowflake when we found out the Sugar Creek school was going to get to close too. Of course, we could have burned wood, but the school board decided not to let us do that so we almost *had* to go on a vacation to show the coal miners how much we appreciated their not working. My parents, especially Mom, felt sorry for the coal miners' wives, who might not have enough money to buy their groceries and she hoped the miners' little children wouldn't have to go hungry.

Dad didn't say much except that coal mining was very hard work and any man who had to work all day in a mine wearing out his muscles and sometimes his lungs away down under the earth, certainly ought to have a good salary—as much as his boss could afford to pay.

Anyway the coal miners' strike was good for

13

the Sugar Creek Gang, so as soon as our school closed, we quick packed up and away we went.

On the way we stopped to see some important places, one of which was Turkey Run State Park, which in the summertime is one of the most beautiful places in the world, having deep canyons and gorges cut right through sandstone rock.

"We'll have to come here some time in the summer," Dad said, "when old Sugar Creek isn't all chained with ice and snow."

"*Sugar* Creek!" Dragonfly exclaimed. "Is *that* Sugar Creek?"

"Sure," Poetry said—he being in the back seat of our car with Dragonfly and me. "Don't you know your geography?"

"What's geography got to do with Sugar Creek?" Dragonfly asked, he not being very good in that subject.

Poetry answered, "Don't be so dumb; don't you know that Sugar Creek is the very center of the geographical world? Anybody knows that!"

Sometimes Poetry used such an argumentative tone of voice that it made me want to talk back even when I agreed with him, but this time I didn't let myself, so I said to Dragonfly, "Sure, anybody knows that"—which anybody does.

The next place we stopped was at one of my cousins' houses, which wasn't very far from Turkey Run. There we left Charlotte Ann, so the coal miners' strike would be good for Mom as well as for the rest of us—because when Charlotte Ann's around and not asleep, there isn't a moment of peace for anybody—she being what is called a normal two-year-old baby girl, which means it is very hard on her nerves to have to be quiet.

As soon as Mom and Charlotte Ann had finished crying, we started on—Dad driving a little faster to make up for lost time, which Mom said wasn't lost.

When we w e r e going through Vincennes, Indiana, Dad reminded us that it was the first capital of what our history books called Indian Territory. Say, when we crossed a big river to go into Illinois, Dragonfly looked out and down at the water and said, "Old Sugar Creek's water certainly looks good this far from home."

"You're crazy," Poetry said. "That's the Wabash River."

"I know it," Dragonfly said, "but our geography book has a map in it that shows Sugar Creek empties its water into the Wabash away back up there somewhere not far from Turkey Run, and some of that water down there is Sugar Creek water."

It kind of tickled me that Dragonfly was smart enough to think of that—and of course he was right. Some of the water in the Wabash River had been given to it absolutely free by good old Sugar Creek.

At a smallish little town called Samburg in Tennessee, which we drove out of our way to go through the next day, Dad stopped while we looked at a terribly big lake and told us, "That's Reelfoote Lake, boys. It was made by an earthquake in 1811—supposed to be the biggest earthquake America ever had."

It certainly was the strangest-looking lake I ever saw. It looked like there were maybe ten thousand old tree stumps sticking up all over it. There were also a lot of whole trees, especially cypress trees, making it look like a forest growing in a lake. Part of it looked like a Sugar Creek cemetery with a lot of black ghosts standing around in it.

"That's probably some of Sugar Creek's water," Dragonfly said. "Let's go in swimming."

"Don't carry a good joke too far," Poetry said scowling.

But Dad heard Dragonfly and said, "You're right, Roy"—that b e i n g Dragonfly's civilized name. "At the time of the earthquake the Mississippi River had something like an epileptic fit. Its water backed up and filled all the huge cracks and crevices which the earthquake had made. Some of that water was probably Sugar Creek water because as you know Sugar Creek flows into the Wabash and the Wabash into the Ohio and the Ohio into the Mississippi. Yes, that's probably partly Sugar Creek water."

All of a sudden Little Jim, who had been beside me, broke away, made a dash down to the lake, scooped up a double handful of water and with a grin on his mouselike face tossed the water up in the air over our heads. A second later some of it spattered on my freckled face while he yelled with a happy, Little-Jim grin on his face, "Hurrah, it's raining Sugar Creek water!"

It was time to drive on, so we did, not stopping at any place very important until we got to Houston,

the largest city in Texas, where there was a
natural history museum and a zoo, called the
Hermann Park Zoo.

2

It had been a long time since any of us had been to a zoo, so because most of us were tired almost to death of riding and wanted to take a walk, our two sets of parents drove us out to the zoo where we walked around the grounds and saw a lot of wild animals and snakes and very strange-looking birds. It was more fun than a barrel of monkeys to watch everything, especially the different kinds of monkeys. There wasn't any snow on the ground so we walked around with our coats off like everyone else was doing and felt as warm as if we were in the middle of a Sugar Creek summer. Dragonfly wasn't sneezing a bit and felt wonderful.

I noticed lots of people were walking around looking at the different exhibits, but the thing I liked best, for a while anyway, was a very small lake with palm trees and a banana tree growing on a little island in the middle of it. All around the shore and on the island were great big, ugly-looking alligators sleeping in the sun.

That reminded Poetry of a poem, which he started to quote:

> Lazy bones, sleepin' in the sun,
> How you 'spect to get your day's work done?

Some of the alligators were sleeping only a few feet from us on the other side of a low fence which they could have knocked down if they had wanted to. Maybe they would have if they had been hungry for fresh boy meat. Circus yelled down at one that was about eight feet long and said, "Wake up, you lazy, good-for-nothing *mississippiensis!*"

"Wake up—*what?*" Dragonfly wanted to know.

And Circus answered, "That is the scientific name for him."

Mississippiensis certainly was a terrible-looking animal, having a very broad head with a rounded snout and black all over except for some very dull yellow markings the color of a boy's faded straw hat after it has been in the sun and wind for maybe five summers.

"How would you like to get a fish like that on your line when we go fishing down on the Gulf of Mexico?" Big Jim asked Little Jim.

That little guy looked up from where he was standing beside me and said, "*That* is no fish, that is a *crocodillian reptile*," which I happened to know it was, from a book I had in my library at home. "Besides," Little Jim added, "alligators don't live in the Gulf of Mexico but in swamps and rivers," which I also knew probably before Little Jim did.

"How about the Rio Grande River?" Poetry asked. "We might go fishing there too."

None of us knew for sure whether there were alligators in the Rio Grande but I sort of hoped there wouldn't be because a *wild* alligator might be hungrier than one that was sleeping in the Houston sun acting like my dad does sometimes when he has just had a chicken dinner and wants to take a nap, and Mom wants him to help with the dishes and I get to help instead.

Right that second Dragonfly started to get a messed-up expression on his face. He quick grabbed his nose, looked around worriedly and sneezed in the direction of a pen of wolves and coyotes. Circus looked too and let out a fierce wild-sounding, high-pitched wail that was supposed to be like a wolf making a wolf call. That started things. In a second there was a wild hullabaloo of wolves' and coyotes' voices howling and yelping and making a bloodcurdling chorus of cries.

Well, Hermann Park Zoo was certainly a very interesting zoo to visit and it felt good to be walking around without our coats and hats. It made me feel sorry for all the people at Sugar Creek who had to live in cold weather.

That night when we were all in our motel and I was lying in a bed with Little Jim in another bed about four feet from mine, all of a sudden he started to mumble something in his sleep. I had been lying there looking up at a very bright moon, which was shining on me through a window, and I had been listening to the rasping sound which the wind made blowing through the leaves of a palm tree. One of the long, turkey-feather-shaped leaves of the palm was brushing against the tiled roof of our cabin.

I strained my ears to hear what Little Jim might be dreaming about. He groaned like he was having trouble of some kind. Then his bedsprings jiggled like he was turning over, which he did with an impatient flip-flop like a boy does when something wakes him up too early in the morning and he doesn't want to get up. I heard him let out an extra-long tired-out sigh and in a jiffy he was breathing a very regular noisy-boy kind of breathing, which meant he was asleep again.

Generally, not very much can wake me up once I drop off to sleep, but it had been such a wonderful trip so far, seeing so many things and having so much fun. Also it seemed wonderful to be in a warm country right here in America. I got to thinking about all the wild animals I had seen in their cages and I was glad the Sugar Creek Gang didn't have to live in cages but were as free as a lot of red-winged blackbirds which in the summertime make their nests along the Sugar Creek bank and whose songs are so pretty to listen to, it almost makes a boy's heart hurt to hear them.

Up above the telephone-pole-shaped palm tree outside I could see—when the wind whipped the leaves around just right—the whole big, round face of the moon which right that same minute was maybe shining down on a lot of terribly cold snowdrifts and bare trees up north and also on old frozen-faced Sugar Creek itself.

I drifted off into a strange sort of dream. A great big ugly, scaly, black alligator with straw-hat-colored markings on him raised his head up out of Sugar Creek, opened his mouth and made a lunge for Little Jim, who was in swimming with the rest of us. It was a terrible dream and I was still scared when I woke up. Little Jim was there in his bed beside me still sleeping, so right away I felt good again. When I told Dad about my dream he sort of laughed and said, "That is because you ate too big a supper."

It took us a whole day of fast driving to get from Houston to the Rio Grande Valley, that very pretty territory at the bottom of the United States map. All of a sudden we were there and our cars were flying along a paved road with palm trees on each side, also orange and lemon and grapefruit groves.

Dragonfly and Poetry were in the back seat with me at the time. "Look," Dragonfly said, "there are a lot of people working out in the field."

"Wetbacks," my dad said from behind the steering wheel. "There are about three hundred and fifty thousand of them working in the Rio Grande Valley between Brownsville and El Paso."

"What's a wetback?" Dragonfly asked.

Dad, who always seemed to know something about everything because he was always reading and learning, said, "A wetback is a Mexican who has entered our country illegally by wading or swimming across the Rio Grande. They get jobs here and make a lot more money than they can in their own country. Some of them go back to Mexico later where they spend the money."

Poetry and Dragonfly and I were interested in something else just then while Mom and Dad talked about different things—I didn't realize what kind of things until I heard Dad say, "They found thirty-eight dead wetbacks in the Rio Grande in one year."

Mom gasped and I sat up straight to listen, especially since Poetry's fat elbow pushed itself against my ribs and he raised a mysterious finger to his lips.

I spoke up quick and said to Dad, "What's that?"

"Oh, nothing," Mom said—my folks not remembering I wasn't little anymore and not wanting me to hear what they called "gruesome."

"Did they drown trying to swim across?" Dragonfly asked, he being too little to hear about such things himself.

Dad must have decided we could stand it so he said, "They were murdered."

"*Murdered!*" Mom exclaimed and the way she said it made me think maybe she was too little herself.

"It's this way," Dad explained. "It seems that after a wetback has been in our country for a while—long enough to have a nice little sum of money—he tries to go back secretly, swimming or wading or being rowed across the river. Evidently some criminals were hiding out along the river watching for any wetbacks who were going home. They waylaid them at the border either on the Texas or on the Mexico side, robbed and killed them, and threw their bodies into the river."

"How did they kill them?" Dragonfly asked from beside me.

"In different ways," Dad said and changed the subject. "Look, here's where we turn off to go to McAllen. This road goes on to Brownsville."

Dad slowed down and turned right and away we went west on a road that was numbered 83 and 281. We went zipping along between orange and grapefruit orchards with tall palm trees on either side of the road like maples and elms border the roads back home. Our car window was open and the cool, friendly breeze that came in felt wonderful on my warm freckled face. The towns seemed so close together that you were in the middle of the next one almost before you left the end of the last one—different towns such as Mercedes, Welasco, Donna and Pharr—and then in a little while we were in McAllen where I noticed that nearly most of the people were Mexicans with dark black hair, and everybody was busy and looked happy, and the stores were nearly all new.

Dad drove straight to a hotel, which was named Casa de Palmas, which means "House of Palms." He and Mom and Dragonfly's parents went in to register while we six boys climbed out of the cars and roamed kind of bashfully around, looking at different things, especially at the big palm trees and at the great big red double-sized poinsettias blossoming at the tops of flower stalks which were higher than our heads. We also looked at a beautiful vine plant with brilliant purplish-red flowers which Little Jim, who had a book of garden flowers at home, said was Bougainvillaea.

Circus didn't seem very happy. He had a dark scowl on his face so I said, " 'Smatter, Circus?"

He said gloomily, "Who wants to climb a palm tree?" As you know, Circus would rather climb a tree than do anything else and if ever we don't know where he is at Sugar Creek, we always look up when we try to find him.

"Yeah," Poetry said, being so fat he couldn't climb one anyway, "who does?"

We were standing right beside a tall palm tree whose smooth, gray trunk zoomed straight up almost forty feet before there were any limbs; in fact there weren't any limbs at all but only a lot of great big, dark green fan-shaped leaves as big as an elephant's ears in the Hermann Park Zoo. Circus was right, I thought. A palm tree might be very pretty to look at in a picture book, or just to look at, but no tree seemed like a good tree to a boy if he couldn't climb it or swing on its branches

or pick mulberries or cherries or something in it—
and you couldn't do that to the prettiest, straightest
palm tree in the world.

Dragonfly's dad and Dad had arranged for all
of us six boys to sleep in an apartment over somebody's garage away out at the edge of town not far
from what is called the "brush," which is the name
of the very thick forestlike woods which grow
wild all along the Rio Grande River. The garage
and apartment belonged to some man who had
lived at Sugar Creek a long time ago before any
of our gang was born and who had been a special
friend of Dragonfly's parents and had been trying
to get them to move down there in the first place.
They had fixed up enough beds for all of the
gang to sleep in.

Mom didn't exactly want to stay in the fancy
hotel which Dad had picked out for her, but Dad
had decided she had to. "You're going to live in
luxury and be waited on and not have to cook a
single meal or wash a dish for a whole week,"
Dad had said.

Even before we had left home Dad had
told me about it, saying, "It's this way, son.
A man who really loves his wife ought to see

29

to it that she gets a little variety in life, even if it seems to cost a lot of money, because a wife is worth more than the money it costs to take care of her. There is nothing a man can buy that is more important than his wife's goodwill and good health; and your mother needs a vacation pretty badly—a lot more than she thinks she does. She has worked very hard all these years, and I can tell it is beginning to get on her nerves. We have a pretty wonderful wife and mother, Bill—you know that, don't you?"

He and I had been out in our barn at the time and Mom had just called us to supper. I had known she was that kind of a mother all my life without anybody having to tell it to me, but when Dad said that like that I looked up at his big bushy eyebrows and his gray-green eyes under them, and I think maybe for the first time I realized that Mom belonged to both of us. It was up to us to look after her and take care of her and not let her work too hard and to see to it that she didn't have too much to worry about. Also it seemed like maybe I ought to try to be a better boy than I had been.

"Sure," I said to Dad, and that evening when

I had gone up to our haymow to throw down the hay for old Topsy and the cows, I stayed up there a little longer than I sometimes do. As you maybe know, away up in a far corner of our haymow where there is a crack between a log, I had a very special place in the hay where sometimes when I felt lonesome and also when I was especially happy inside, I liked to go. I would take out from the crack in the log my little brown leather New Testament, which I kept there, and would read a verse or two or more. Then as quick as anything I'd drop down on both knees in the hay and pray something or other to God, whom I liked even better than I liked my folks and who had made all the world we lived in and had sent His Son to be our Saviour.

I can't remember exactly what I prayed that late afternoon, but there was sort of an ache in my heart because maybe I had caused my mother too much worry that summer and winter. So I asked God to help me to do something about myself and to make me kinder to my mother; also to help me actually look for things I could do to help her around the house and yard without being told to. I felt like I wanted to be as kind to her as Dad was.

3

WELL, THERE WE WERE in the Rio Grande Valley, all six of the Sugar Creek Gang and four of our parents, and I just knew something absolutely very, very different was going to happen to us. We were going fishing in the Gulf of Mexico and visit Old Point Lighthouse at Port Isabel. Also we were going to cross over the Rio Grande to Old Mexico itself and see all of the different things. You know, we might run into some kind of a dangerous experience with a wetback or a criminal of some kind.

That night when the gang was sitting and lying and sprawling around on bunks and chairs and gliders on our upstairs apartment porch chattering about our trip and the wonderful, warm weather and planning tomorrow's adventures,

Poetry, who was on the glider beside me helping me make it swing, sort of leaned his head over on my shoulder and whispered against my cheek, saying, "If we expect to really have an exciting adventure down here, we may have to go out and look for one. Adventures are funny things. They don't come hunting you up—you have to go where they happen."

I was kind of sleepy and not too interested in having any kind of adventure right that minute. Certainly I didn't want to start out that night in a strange country like Texas, especially when our apartment wasn't too far from a regular jungle of strange trees, bushes, prickly-pear cactus, what is called "cat's claw," and mesquite and stuff— the kind of growth you have to watch out for all the time when you walk through it or you'll get scratched or stuck or clawed. Certainly I didn't want to look for any adventures in the dangerous dark, which it probably would be that close to the Mexican border.

So I grunted and answered Poetry, saying, "Let's all get to bed so we'll feel like a million dollars in the morning and be ready for our trip into Old Mexico."

"Shhh!" Poetry said, "don't mention money out here on this open porch. You remember they throw dead bodies in the Rio Grande River after they have robbed and killed them."

"They just do that to wetbacks," I said, and Little Jim heard me say that and spoke up and said, "What's a wetback?"

I realized then that Little Jim had not been in the car with us when we had talked about them. So pretty soon all of us were discussing wetbacks. I explained to Little Jim and the others that wetbacks are Mexican citizens who, because they can make more money working in America or maybe because they don't have any work in their hometowns, wade or swim or row across the Rio Grande to get a job here.

"Why don't they just go right down to the bridge and *walk* across?" Little Jim asked.

"They aren't supposed to work in America unless they are American citizens," Big Jim said, "which you aren't if you are born in Mexico. If the United States let all of the Mexicans who wanted to, come over here, there wouldn't be any jobs left for the people who are already citizens. Then maybe the Mexicans would work all summer and make a lot of money and take it back to Mexico and spend it there instead of here in our country."

I didn't understand it very well myself because it sounded like some things we were supposed to study in our history and civics books in school and I wasn't very good in those subjects, but I remembered what Dad had said in the car in the afternoon so I kept on explaining it.

"Sometimes when they try to go back across the river at night, robbers waylay them and take their money. Sometimes they kill them and throw their bodies in the Rio Grande. One year the police found thirty-eight different bodies of people who—"

That was as far as I got when Big Jim interrupted me with "Shhh! Let's don't talk about stuff like that before going to bed or somebody will have a nightmare."

If there is anything I don't like more than I don't like anything else it is to be shushed right in the middle of something I am saying, so I said to Big Jim, "Oh, of course, if you're scared or nervous or—"

Then Big Jim shushed me again and said,

"Listen, everybody; somebody's singing or something."

So I shushed myself and listened, expecting to hear some pretty Mexican music but instead it was a quartet of men's voices singing a very cheerful gospel song, which we sometimes sing on Sunday in the Sugar Creek Church and it was:

> I won't have to cross Jordan alone
> Jesus died for my sins to atone.

"It's a sound truck," Big Jim said. "It's coming nearer"—which it was.

Because every single one of the Sugar Creek Gang liked to hear gospel songs and hymns, we all kept still and listened. As quick as the quartet finished, I heard a loud, amplified voice saying, "BEGINNING SUNDAY NIGHT IN THE BIG TENT ON THE HIGHWAY BETWEEN DONNA AND PHARR. BE SURE TO HEAR THE RIO GRANDE QUARTET AND THE BOY EVANGELIST, DAVID MULDER. EVERYONE INVITED. SEE ALSO THE CHRISTIAN MOTION PICTURE 'DUST OR DESTINY.' ADMISSION FREE."

All of a sudden I got a warm feeling in my heart because my folks had taken me to church ever since I was old enough to be carried there and I was glad the people clear down here, halfway to the bottom of the world, were going to hear the gospel too. I had never heard what is called a "boy preacher" and I wished the gang could get to go tomorrow night to hear him.

Also I would like to see an honest-to-goodness Christian motion picture in a big tent. Maybe you know that none of the Collins family ever went to the Sugar Creek theater, because Dad and Mom both have told me so many times I can quote it from memory, "The motion picture industry as a whole is rotten, Bill, and even though there may be a good picture once in a while, we, as Christians, do not believe we should support it." Also our minister says that people who go to shows all the time never care very much about getting anybody to become a Christian, so if I got to see an honest-to-goodness *Christian* picture it would be fine.

The sound of the sound truck faded away as it went on down the street.

"What's the *Jordan?*" Dragonfly asked all of a sudden like he had just that second heard the quartet singing "I Won't Have to Cross Jordan Alone."

Poetry said, "That's the name of a river in Palestine."

"Was somebody afraid he would have to go across all by himself?" Dragonfly asked, being slower even than I am to understand things like that.

All of us were quiet for a while. Even though every single one of us liked to listen to other people talk about things the Bible teaches, still we were kind of bashful about doing it ourselves; but I knew that if our minister had been with us and Dragonfly had asked that question, he'd probably have said, "In the song, the Jordan means the river of death. The man who wrote it meant that when he died the Saviour would meet him on the bank of the river and go across with him." In fact, Big Jim himself said that very thing a jiffy later.

Then Dragonfly asked an ignorant question which got me started thinking about the Rio Grande and wetbacks again. "When we die will we wade across or swim across, or will there be a boat or a canoe?"

Even Little Jim knew better than to ask a

dumb question like that because he piped up right then in his small friendly voice and said, "It's not an actual river!"—which anybody knows it isn't.

Anyway it was time for us all to get into our nightclothes and also into our bunks. I was so sleepy by that time that I was sure if my eyes ever went shut without my knowing it, it would be morning before I opened them again.

Right after I had finished saying a quiet goodnight prayer and just as Poetry finished his, he and I slipped out onto the moonlit porch again—the weather being so warm we could be out there in our pajamas without even feeling chilly. I noticed that the moon's round face was as clean and white as it had been in Houston last night. It seemed wonderful to think that right below us on the lawn was an honest-to-goodness orange tree with honest-to-goodness oranges on it. Tomorrow maybe we could pick one off apiece and eat it.

There was a warm breeze blowing and the extra-long branches of the palm tree in the center of the lawn were swinging from side to side making a very happy swishing sound as they rubbed together. It was like the sound the waves of a lake make washing and washing against a sandy shore.

I had heard that same friendly over-and-over-again sound many a summer moonlit night on vacations the gang had taken in northern Minnesota, which I have told you about in some of the other Sugar Creek Gang books.

All of a sudden Poetry beside me said, "Listen."

I listened but couldn't hear anything except the wind. "It's the wind in the palm tree," I said and he said, "I know it."

Because nearly everything Poetry ever saw or heard or tasted or smelled or felt reminded him of a poem, he started quoting part of one right that minute—one we had all memorized in one of our Sugar Creek school books which goes something like this:

> The husky, rusty rustle
> Of tassels of the corn.

For the first time in my life I realized that whoever wrote that poem had made a mistake, because anybody who knows anything about a cornfield knows it isn't the *tassels* of the corn that make the rustling sounds in the wind, because they are too far apart to rub against each other;

but it is the big, long, sword-shaped *blades* brushing against each other.

So I said to Poetry, "If James Whitcomb Riley had lived down here, he could have said, 'The husky, rusty rasping of the palm leaves of the palm'—or something."

Just thinking about the tall, dark green, grown-up corn that lives in the fields up north in the summer and also thinking about the woods where maple, elm, ash, walnut, linden, and all kinds of other friendly trees grow, the kind a boy can climb and have fun in, made me lonesome for home. It didn't seem right for it to be summer weather in the winter.

But the moon looked just like it did back home and also it felt the same way to be sleepy down along the Rio Grande as it did along Sugar Creek. So Poetry and I right away left the moon to take care of itself and went inside where most of the rest of us were already asleep.

In what seemed like only a jiffy it was morning again, our first morning in the Rio Grande Valley. Right in the middle of the kind of noise a gang of boys makes when it starts waking up and getting up, I heard a bird outside making a very friendly, cheerful bird call that sounded like "cheo-cheo-chehoo-cheo."

Little Jim who was already up and out on the porch called back in to us, "Hey, you guys, it's a *cardinal!*"

In a fast jiffy I was out there with him with only one slipper on and my green-striped pajamas also still on. I got there just in time to see what looked like a flash of red fire in the top of the orange tree before it shot like an arrow right through the warm blue-skied weather straight toward some kind or other of a tree in the direction of the "brush," which was also in the direction of the Rio Grande River.

"If a cardinal flies across the river into Mexico will somebody make him fly back again and live *here?*" Dragonfly asked.

Circus heard him say that and answered, "Birds don't have any nationality, they just belong to the world."

"Where do we eat?" Poetry wanted to know and so did the rest of us.

Big Jim had a map of the town, so pretty soon we were all on our way to the hotel where we were supposed to meet the four parents who were supposed to be our chaperons while we were down there.

While we were half-walking and half-running beside and behind and in front of one another through the very interesting townful of Americans and Mexicans, I thought how much the Mexicans seemed like suntanned white people, only they had the kind of a tan that would not have to have sunshine all the time or it would fade.

I was remembering Mom's yesterday's last words to me when I had told her good night at the hotel before the gang had left for its apartment: "Be a good boy, Bill—like you sometimes are when you don't have a chaperon."

There had been a twinkle in her eye which meant she liked me but didn't quite trust me one hundred per cent.

"What's a chaperon?" Dragonfly had asked and Poetry, trying to be funny, answered for me, saying, "It's what the rest of us are glad we don't have two apiece of."

When we got to the hotel desk I asked the clerk to phone the room of Mr. and Mrs. Theodore Collins of Sugar Creek to tell them there were six boys in the lobby.

A friendly, middle-aged woman who was a telephone operator, picked up a plunger the size of one-fourth of a boy's pencil, which was fastened to a long rubber tube, plugged it into one of about two hundred small sockets on the switchboard in front of her and pressed a buzzer, waited a jiffy for Dad or Mom to answer and said, "There are six hungry boys waiting for you in the lobby."

"*Terribly* hungry," Poetry said.

"*Terribly* hungry," the middle-aged woman repeated into the mouthpiece of her telephone and Poetry's face turned as red as the red side of a maiden blush apple from the tree in his backyard at home.

"They will be down in about ten minutes," the telephone operator said. "You are to wait outside in the patio."

"Would you please call Dragonfly's parents, too?" I asked, and the middle-aged woman's mischievous eyes flashed from one to the other of our kind of homely faces like she had never seen such different-looking faces in her life—and maybe she hadn't, and she hadn't missed much either. There was Big Jim's face, which was the oldest-looking one with an almost moustache on his upper lip; Circus' face that looked like one of the chimpanzees in the Hermann Park Zoo at Houston; Poetry's face looking like a full moon with a fat nose in the middle and with eyebrows that grew together in the center just above the bridge of his nose; Dragonfly's face with a crooked nose, which he could see the south end of without looking in the mirror if he would shut his right eye; Little Jim's friendly, innocent mouse-shaped face; and finally mine with its very ordinary nose which even in the winter had a lot of unnecessary freckles on it.

"Are you Dragonfly?" the telephone operator asked, looking right straight at Dragonfly himself.

He grinned with a scowl on his forehead and answered, "Yes, ma'am," and swallowed a big lump in his throat.

"Your chaperons' names are Mr. and Mrs. Gilbert, aren't they?"

Pretty soon while we were still waiting for the Gilbert and Collins parents, the gang was walking around on one of the hotel patios, which was like a large lawn with lawn furniture and colored outdoor umbrellas, only where the grass was supposed to be there was a beautifully designed tiled flooring like the kind Poetry's parents have in their recreation room in the basement of their house.

"Look," Little Jim said, "yonder is a whole lot of live fishing poles."

We all looked where he was pointing and sure enough at the farther end of the tiled patio on the back side of what looked like the latticed backdrop of a stage was a cluster of maybe thirty tall, green bamboo trees, most of them just the right size for fishing poles.

There were a lot of flowers and trees and shrubs on a pretty lawn on the other side of another patio on the other side of the hotel; also across a paved street in a park, which had a bandstand in the middle, there were many other flowers such as oleander, bougainvillaea, roses, and poinsettias.

"Look," Circus said, "there are a lot of melons growing on a tree"—which they were *not* but only looked like it and we found out later they were called papaya. About fifteen muskmelon-looking fruits were hanging in a large cluster about eight feet from the ground.

Pretty soon Dad came out onto the patio. "Boy, oh boy! Whew! Land sakes!" I thought.

Who was that tall woman in the extra-pretty summer suit walking along with him with her hand resting in the crook of his arm? It couldn't be, it just *couldn't* be, and yet it *had* to be 'cause it was! It was my very own mom dressed up in a brand new toast-colored suit with a daffodil-colored blouse and a frilly collar which had a neck shaped like a short letter V. Also she was wearing a new kind of perky hat with flowers on it, which made her look even more than ever special. She was wearing high-heeled green shoes.

4

I MUST HAVE STOPPED stock-still and stared at my
different-looking mother. She didn't even look as
big around as she did at home. For a half second
I couldn't believe it was her until Dragonfly beside me sneezed and I remembered he was allergic
to Mom's new face powder. Then my mixed-up
mind found my lost voice and I said, "How do
you do, parents!"

Dad himself looked dressed up. He had on
a noisy necktie that had a hand-painted tall palm
tree on it with a pretty green lake in the back-
ground with a sailboat in the middle of the lake.

"The name is Collins," Dad said in a mischievous, dignified voice. "Mr. and Mrs. Theodore

Collins of Sugar Creek." He held out his hand as if he was meeting me for the first time in my life.

Not to be outdone by him I took his hand and shook it and also Mrs. Collins' hand.

Even if I hadn't seen Mom or heard her Sugar Creek voice, I would have known her just by looking at and feeling her hand because it was one of the same hands she used when she did the work at home, such as peeling potatoes, washing dishes —while I wiped them—also the same hand she had used to stroke my forehead once that very same winter when I had been sick in bed with a high fever and she sat beside me like she always does when I have to go to bed with a cold or something. It was also the same hand which, a couple of times or more, had given me a few sad spankings.

Pretty soon all of us were in the hotel's ritzy dining room waiting for breakfast.

"Quite a nice change," Mom said to Dragonfly's mom when we were all seated around a large table. "It feels good to be waited on for once."

Dad heard her say that and caught my eye and I could tell by the way he winked at me he was feeling fine because he and I could give Mom a winter vacation away from home with nothing for her to do.

All ten of us were seated at one big table in the end of the ritzy dining room and were waiting to be waited on by two white-coated Mexican boys.

I put on my mom's favorite table manners, which she had made for me herself. Because most of the rest of the gang were half-scared or half-bashful or both, we all behaved like all our parents thought we should.

With so many people all around us, I wondered what Dad would do about the blessing before we ate. I knew if he asked it out loud it would make everybody else in the dining room stop and look and listen like we were some kind of odd people, which people do when you bow your head to pray in a public eating place, because most other people start right in eating without praying, like cows do—cows not knowing any better, Dad says.

Pretty soon ten platters of buckwheat pancakes came steaming in. It was a pretty sight to see them, not only when you looked around the table at them but also when you saw them reflected in the very large six-foot-by-eight-foot mirror which was on the wall across from where I sat.

While I was still watching us in the mirror and while the two white-coated Mexican boys hurried back and forth around us, I noticed that Mom's green hat was the same color as the six or seven philodendron plants, which were growing in the same number of copper flower pots on the branches of an iron tree that was standing in front of the mirror. The color of the hat and the philodendron plant leaves was the same as a maple leaf in the woods back home. In the mirror I could even recognize the back of Mom's green hat and her head.

Just then Dad said to all of us, "Let's each one ask his own blessing quietly," then he bowed his head first and right away we all did the same thing. In a jiffy our ten quiet prayers were finished and we were all sawing away on our pancakes.

Dragonfly's mom seemed even more bashful than she thought *he* was, because the Gilbert family hardly ever ate any meals anywhere except at home. I noticed she kept watching her boy with a now-and-then worried look on her face to see if he was using good manners, which if he didn't, it might mean she was to blame.

But Dragonfly was perfect. He had to sneeze only once, which he did very politely into his handkerchief while he turned his face to one side like he was used to it and said, "Excuse me, please," which we all did without saying so.

"There was a time," Dad said to Dragonfly's dad across the corner of the table, "When I hesitated about bowing my head over my plate in a public dining room for fear of what people would think, but I don't feel that way about it anymore. I always begin my silent prayer by saying, 'May somebody with a heavy heart see me and be reminded that there is a God who loves him and to whom he can tell his troubles.' "

It was certainly different, eating breakfast in that fancy dining room with all the windows wide open and the cool breeze blowing in and birds singing outside, but the gang didn't seem to be enjoying it as much as our chaperons were. We were eager to get started on some kind of an adventure where we could use our muscles to save somebody from some danger or something.

Dad and Dragonfly's dad had already decided

to spend part of their morning looking at citrus groves. Mom and Dragonfly's mom were going to "meander around the stores awhile" as Mom expressed it. We, the gang, could do anything we wanted to but had to be ready to meet at the hotel in one of the patios at 11:00, then we would all drive across the Rio Grande to Old Mexico and maybe have a Mexican dinner in a Mexican cafe. Also I hoped we would run into an honest-to-goodness adventure.

We stumbled onto the beginning of a very different kind of adventure that very afternoon. We had been in Mexico for maybe an hour driving and walking around and looking at the different interesting and educational things such as a very pretty, block-square, flower-filled, tree-shaded park, right in the middle of the town. We saw also a very gruesome-looking cemetery with the graves only a couple of feet apart, each of them having a black wooden cross for a marker with a wreath of dead or dying flowers hanging across the upright of the cross. There was a new cemetery right beside the older one, which had a sign in Spanish above the gate. Big Jim translated it for us and it was "Modern Funerals, Day or Night."

Also our two other chaperons visited what they called "exciting shops" and acted like two grown-up schoolgirls who were having the time of their lives looking at things and also buying stuff such as two baskets, a couple of head scarves and some fancy drinking glasses.

After our Mexican dinner and before going back across the border, Mom and Dragonfly's mom decided they wanted to look around in other exciting shops near the park, so Dad and Dragonfly's dad drove round and round looking for a place to park but couldn't find one until we came to an old Mexican church.

The very second we stopped and started to pile out, a bright-eyed, sincere-looking Mexican boy about my size came hurrying up, saying, "Watch your car—fi' cents," only it sounded like "wash" your car.

Dad looked at the boy with his bushy-eyebrow-shaded eyes, smiled at him from under his reddish-brown moustache and said, "Sure," and handed him a whole quarter.

"*Muchas gracias*, senor. Thank you!" the boy said politely.

Our two mothers hurried across to the exciting

shops while our two dads went to wait for them on one of the benches in the park. That left the gang alone for a while, which we would rather be anyway.

We looked at the store windows for a while and finally went in an interesting-looking saddle shop. When we came out into the bright sunshine where our car was, Dad and Mom and Dragonfly's mom and dad were just coming across the street from the park.

"Where's the boy I gave the quarter to?" Dad said, looking all around while we all started to do the same thing.

But do you know what? That black-haired, brown-skinned, friendly Mexican boy had disappeared.

Dad laughed a little, then said, "Maybe he ran off somewhere to spend his quarter."

In a few jiffies we would be on our way to the bridge that spans the Rio Grande and soon would be back in the United States. Dragonfly's mom had bought a colored basket of some kind so his dad put it in the trunk of their car and locked it. I remembered the lock on the trunk of our car had been broken in a sort of half accident back home when Mom had been accidentally driving backward one day—and we hadn't had a chance to get the lock fixed before coming south.

At the river we were stopped by some officers who were stopping all cars because it was a toll bridge and we had to pay a few cents apiece to ride across it.

Also we had to answer different questions. Dragonfly and his parents and Big Jim and Circus were in the car ahead of ours. They got past the customs OK, then came our turn.

"Are you all American citizens?" the officer asked us and Poetry and I answered, "Yes."

He gave us all a quick look-over, winked at Poetry and Little Jim and me in the back seat, and said to Mom and Dad in the front seat, "Did you buy anything in Mexico valued at more than one hundred dollars?"

"Only a few useless trinkets," Dad said mischievously and Mom held up some things she had in her lap.

"Anything in the trunk of your car?"

And that is where we had the beginning of our adventure.

5

POETRY AND I had to get out to show the man there wasn't anything in our trunk—like Big Jim and Circus had done just ahead of us—only they had found Dragonfly's mom's new basket in their trunk.

Say, I guess I never got such a different kind of surprise in my life when I lifted up our trunk with its smashed lock. I knew there was an old robe in it, which we had used to cover up some of our luggage when we drove down to the Rio Grande Valley to keep the dust off it, but that was all—only it *wasn't*. There was something covered up under the robe and it was *alive!* I knew because I saw it move; in fact, right that second I saw five brown, bare toes of a boy's bare foot, just before it disappeared under the edge of the robe.

The officer saw it too and yanked off the blanket and what to my wondering eyes should appear but a boy, who was the owner of the five bare toes. It was Dad's twenty-five-cent Mexican boy, whom we had last seen in front of the church. He was all curled up in as small a ball as he could curl himself into.

Right away the officer started talking something in Spanish and the boy started talking back to him in a worried, tearful voice. It sounded like a one-sided argument and because the boy was the littlest of the two I felt sorry for him and wished I could understand Spanish so I could take his part and explain to the officer that whatever he was doing wasn't very bad.

Dragonfly's car was still waiting for ours so in a flash of a jiffy Big Jim and Dragonfly and Circus came tumbling out and back to see what our noisy excitement was all about. Also our two dads came a little slower and for a minute all of us were standing in a mixed-up circle looking into the trunk at the scared Mexican boy who had an expression on his face like a small stray dog that nobody wanted.

It hurt my heart like everything to have to go on across the bridge and leave that very cute-looking boy on his side of the Rio Grande, but the Mexican government couldn't let a boy do a thing like that, Dad explained to us. The boy wouldn't have anyone to look after him in Texas and the state would have to feed him.

"Maybe he already has part of his parents in Texas," Little Jim said as we left the bridge and the brown river behind us.

Poetry spoke up then and suggested, "Maybe he wanted to be a wetback without getting a wet back"—trying to be funny like he sometimes is and not being very, like he sometimes *isn't*.

In my mind's eye I could still see the tears in the boy's eyes. I felt so sorry for him I wished we could have put him right in the car with us and taken him across, but we couldn't.

That night to my absolutely astonishing surprise we saw Dad's twenty-five-cent boy again.

The whole gang of us and our four chaperons had gone to church in the big, brown tent to hear the quartet and the boy evangelist.

Say, that was the most interesting meeting! It was just like the one we had one summer in a large tent back home when most of our Sugar Creek Gang had been saved. That was the time, as you maybe know, when Circus' drunkard dad had started the Christian life. He had been sitting outside the tent in the dark, watching and listening, and when he saw his boy Circus go hurrying down the long, grassy aisle to the platform to confess the Saviour, it had melted his hard, cold heart and he had quickly ducked under the tent's sidewall, scrambled in and onto his feet, still half-drunk and also half-running or staggering down the aisle, crying out loud as he went, and saying, "That's my boy! That's my boy!"

That wonderful night he and Circus and most of us and a lot of other people had gone into what is called an inquiry room beside the platform where all of us had prayed on our knees in the long, mashed-down, brown grass. That had been the beginning of a new life for the Brown family —*Brown* being Circus' last name. After that, in fact almost right away, Circus' dad got a good job and started in making a decent living for his large family of all girls except for one boy.

The boy evangelist's tent was nearly filled with different kinds of people. A lot of them were dressed in their working clothes and nobody seemed to care 'cause nobody was stuck-up. The Mexicans, or the Latin-Americans as Dad called them, and the ordinary Americans and Mexicans and maybe even some wetbacks were all more or less mixed up in the different sections.

It felt good to hear everybody singing the same songs and choruses we used in our own church—some of the numbers being sung in Spanish and some in English. Part of one of the choruses which the black-haired Mexican children on the front rows almost yelled their heads off on, sounded like:

> *Hay perdon por la sangre de Jesus,*
> *Hay perdon por su muerte in la crus—*

which, when they translated it for us, I found out meant:

> There is pardon by the blood of Jesus,
> There is pardon by His death on the cross—

I liked the song right away and in only a few jiffies all the gang, which were sitting in two rows behind and in front of each other away off to one side near one of the tent's sidewalls, were singing like a house afire along with the rest of the people.

It seemed the Mexicans enjoyed singing it even better than we did, especially the children who worked as hard doing it as a gang of boys dashing lickety-sizzle through the woods to see which one could get to the swimming hole first.

It certainly seemed different to hear a boy not more than eleven or twelve years old preach to a tentful of people, quoting dozens of Bible verses, not having to stop to think what to say next, and every now and then slamming home something important—like a boy taking a fierce, hard swing at a hard-pitched baseball and hitting it and knocking a home run and all the people thinking it was grand and yelling for him—only the tentful of different kinds of people didn't yell or shout. But when the boy preacher drove home something extra-important several of the ministers who were sitting on the platform behind him said, "Amen." Also quite a number of the people who were sitting around us did the same thing kind of quietly. "Amen," as you maybe know, means "That's right" or "That's what I think." It almost means about the same as saying "Atta boy" only it is more reverent.

It was when the quartet was singing the same song we had heard last night coming from the sound truck that my curiosity made me begin to look around the tent to see what different people might be thinking. That was when I saw the little twenty-five-cent boy we had found hidden in the broken-locked trunk of our car. When I first glimpsed him, he was crawling in under the tent's sidewall. A second later he was on the edge of a bench beside a Mexican with a moustache. I noticed the man kind of slipped his arm around the boy's shoulders like he knew him and liked him a lot like my dad does me sometimes.

As I said, the quartet was singing "I Won't Have to Cross Jordan Alone" and that had reminded me of the Rio Grande and of the boy in our trunk, so when I looked around and saw him I realized that he had either snitched a ride with somebody else or he had done what thousands of other Mexicans do—waded or swum or been rowed across the river.

Seeing that interesting little guy I almost forgot what else was going on around me. I nudged

Poetry quick in the fat side and jerked my thumb in the direction of the boy. Poetry looked and saw and let out an exclamatory whistle, which he shouldn't have.

I noticed that there was a worried expression on the man's face and that he began whispering something to the boy like a boy's father does when a boy has done something he shouldn't have or maybe when the father thinks he has. Then the man raised his finger to his lips, which meant "Keep still," and he went on paying attention to what was going on on the platform.

Right that second the quartet finished and a middle-aged minister with a forehead that reached all the way back to the back of his head, stood up and in a very kind voice asked if there were any people here who knew in their hearts that nothing could save a person from his sins except the Saviour Himself. "If there is anyone here who knows that and wants to trust Christ alone for his salvation, will he please raise his right hand?"

I noticed that several hands were raised; then the minister asked all of us to shut our eyes and bow our heads, which we did, while he prayed a very nice, friendly prayer asking God to bless the hearts of all the people who had raised their hands.

A little later we all stood up, and anybody who wanted to become a Christian that very night was supposed to go forward and into a small, friendly-looking canvas room beside the platform. And say! What should happen but the man the boy had been sitting beside stepped out into the aisle and was about the third or fourth one to go down to the front where a Mexican minister quick stepped off the platform to meet him, shook hands with him and walked into the inquiry room with him.

I looked around out of the corner of my eye to see what different ones of the gang were thinking. Dragonfly was looking across the tent to where his parents were and I noticed he swallowed kind of hard several times like there might be tears trying to get into his eyes from somewhere and he could keep them from doing it by swallowing, like people do in meetings like that.

Then I did get the surprise of my life. There was a rustling movement over where our folks were and all of a sudden two women, one of them dressed in a new toast-colored suit with a green, flowered hat, and the other Dragonfly's mother, stepped out into the aisle. Mom had her hand on Dragonfly's mom's arm like they were good friends, which they were anyway, and both of them went down to the front and into the little room.

I knew that my mother was already born again so she couldn't be going down there to become a Christian herself, but I didn't get to wonder any farther because right that second I heard a boy sniffling on the other side of Poetry and I knew it was Dragonfly. I also knew it wasn't because he was allergic to anything; then I heard a sort of sob coming from his throat as he sniffled again and muttered in a gulping voice, "That's my mother. She's going to get saved."

Before you could say Jack Robinson, Dragonfly came to quick life, squeezed past Poetry and me and out into the aisle and shot like a spindle-legged arrow straight for the open canvas door of the inquiry room to be with his mother.

I felt myself fighting tears myself. I also felt wonderful inside because I knew Dragonfly was going to have a saved mother. I was glad Mom knew how to pray and that she knew just what Bible verses to show her so she could accept the Saviour, too. I also knew Mom had a small New Testament in her handbag, which she always carried with her even when the handbag was already stuffed with everything you could think of.

I wondered for a jiffy if I ought to go in too just to be with Dragonfly to let him know I was glad for him, but I waited awhile. Then I got another surprise and this time it was the little Mexican boy, who went hurrying down the outside aisle.

Say, Little Jim in the row in front of me made a dive right after him. Then Poetry and I and nearly all the Sugar Creek Gang went too, not to be saved again because you don't have to do that if you are already saved, but mostly because we wanted to be there when Dragonfly's mom became a Christian.

Well, it was really swell and maybe twenty people were saved that night before the meeting was over.

I guess I never saw any prettier sight in my life than all those people in that friendly, little canvas-walled room giving their hearts to God.

Something inside of me felt like a Sugar Creek song—not the kind people sing in church but like the friendly, purling noise which Sugar Creek itself makes when the water from the spring tumbles into it. All these people with happy tears in their eyes made me think of that. I felt as good as I do when I see a fiery red cardinal winging across a sunshiny sky from one tree to another. For some reason it seemed like God, who could make such wonderful things as Sugar Creek and redbirds for a boy to enjoy, was turning loose a whole flock of cardinals to fly around in people's hearts or something.

One of the actually prettiest sights I ever saw in my life though was when Dragonfly's dad and my dad came in too and very quietly knelt down beside our two moms. Dragonfly himself, who had been kneeling beside his mom, seemed a lot smaller than he was. He seemed to want to get a little nearer to what was going on so he snuggled in still closer and tucked his head beneath her arm and pushed the side of his face up close to hers like he wanted to be there for protection.

I was afraid that being so close to my mom he

might get a whiff of her face powder and start a sneezing spell, but he didn't.

Well, while we were in the middle of all that gladness, Dad's little twenty-five-cent boy and his dad disappeared. That is, one minute they were kneeling with the Mexican minister over in a corner, and the next minute they were gone.

Poetry, who was beside me, noticed it first. He nudged his fat elbow into my ribs and whispered against my left cheek, "Hey, Bill! There goes our adventure! Let's go after it or it will be gone forever!"

When Poetry whispered that like that, I quick opened my eyes in the direction my mind told me to just in time to see the boy's bare foot disappearing under the tent flap, which meant that the boy had crawled out and his left foot was the last part of him to leave the tent. The man himself was already gone.

6

WELL, it certainly wasn't the right time and not a very dignified way to leave a gospel meeting, but I almost had to follow Poetry. So in a few jiffies we were both outside the tent.

"There they go," Poetry exclaimed in an excited whisper.

My eyes and ears took in a quick circle of things there in the moonlight—such as a lot of palm trees with their husky, rusty, rasping leaves, a small garage with a tiled roof and behind it the dark beginning of an orange or grapefruit grove. Then I spied the man and the boy as they shot out from behind the garage and made a moonlit dash for the grove.

The next thing I knew I was following Poetry as fast as he could go, right after them.

It was a silly thing to do, I suppose, but I kept on running beside and behind Poetry deeper and deeper into that grapefruit grove—which was the kind of orchard it was. I found that out when I stepped on something large and round about the size of a croquet ball. I stumbled over myself and fell sprawling onto the dusty, cultivated ground. I also fell on several other grapefruit, one of which broke and squished its juice out and up and into my freckled face.

Poetry stooped, caught hold of me and grunted me to my feet.

"We're crazy to be doing this," I said. "How do we know which way they went? Besides we might get lost—oh!" I groaned as a brand new pain shot through my right foot, the one the grapefruit had been under when I stepped on it.

It's never easy to stop Poetry from doing anything exciting he has set his mind on doing. "I'll bet they're both wetbacks," he said, "and have both come into America illegally. Let's find out where they go and report to the police."

I was astonished to hear him say that like that.

I knew from what Dad had told me that there were over 300,000 wetbacks in the United States helping harvest the oranges, grapefruit, lemons, sugar beets, cabbage, lettuce, carrots and stuff. Besides I had also heard Dad say, "That is a problem for the Mexican and United States government to solve," so even though I enjoyed a dangerous mystery as well as Poetry did I certainly didn't like the idea of doing anything to harm that swell-faced little twenty-five-cent guy, who, in the trunk of our car in the afternoon, had looked as scared and lonesome as a little stray dog that nobody wanted, so I answered Poetry by saying, "It's none of our business. Let's go back to the tent before we get lost"—which after a one-sided argument we decided to do, Poetry starting to start back in one direction and I starting to start back in the other and each one of us getting stopped by the other's voice.

"The tent's this way," I exclaimed, surprised at him not knowing which way to go.

"It isn't either, it's *this* way."

"It is *not*," I argued back.

We stayed stopped and looked at each other in our worried, moonlit faces and—well, there we were! Every direction we looked there were grapefruit trees, all of them the same size; and every direction we looked, looked like every other direction. The moon was too straight overhead for us to tell directions by it; besides when we had left the tent we had run in every direction there is, so it looked like we were really lost.

Anyway Poetry was lost and I didn't know for sure which way to go—not quite sure anyway.

How long we might have stayed lost, I don't know, but pretty soon Poetry said, "Listen, I hear music. They're singing in the tent again."

I listened and heard music myself. Somebody was singing a solo. So we started in the direction of the music, glad we knew which way to go to get back to the gang before they would miss us and before two of our chaperons started worrying about us and wondering "What on *earth?*" and "Where?"

I felt pretty good when my sense of hearing told me the music was coming from the same direction as my sense of mind had told me to go in the first place.

"How come they moved the tent over on *that* side of the orchard?" Poetry asked, hating to admit how right *I* had been or maybe hating to admit how wrong *he* had been.

"Yeah, how come?" I said with a little mischievous sarcasm in my voice.

We hurried toward the music. I was puzzled though when about two or three minutes later the music told me we were almost there and there wasn't any tent or any electric light.

A jiffy later Poetry grabbed my arm and stopped me stock-still. "Sh!" he whispered and pulled me behind the branches of a grapefruit tree.

The mystery in his voice and the way he was grasping my arm scattered a shower of shivers all over me. We were within maybe ten yards of the music, which I noticed, when we stopped, was a man's voice with a guitar accompaniment. It seemed like the music was coming from what looked like an old tin-roofed shed of some kind.

"What on *earth?*" I thought with the shower of shivers still falling on me. I realized that our adventure had come to life again. The tree we were hiding behind was at the very edge of the grove, which we had either gone all the way through, or else we had come out on some other different side from the one the tent was on.

The old shed, which was in a little clearing, had a banana tree growing on one side of its open door, and some kind of sweet-smelling, flowering vine was sprawled all over a heart-shaped trellis on the other side. For a second I was glad Dragonfly wasn't there to interrupt our silence by one of his fuzzy sneezes.

There wasn't even a light in the old shed so the door was like a big, black rectangular hole. At first I was sure the music was coming from inside, but a jiffy later I found out it wasn't because right that second Poetry put his lips up close to my ear and whispered, "Look, there's somebody hiding behind the trunk of that palm tree."

I looked toward the palm tree, which was about twenty feet from the shed and saw the shadow of a man there, also a quick rhythmic movement like the movement a person's wrist makes when he is strumming a guitar or a ukulele.

"What do you suppose is going on?" Poetry asked me, but I couldn't even guess. That is, I couldn't at first, but a moment later I saw a light in the shed when somebody struck a match. Quick as a flash the whole inside of the room was alive with light from what looked like a kerosene lamp just like the one we used in our upstairs at home.

"What on *earth?*" I thought. Why, the old shed wasn't a shed at all but was somebody's house, maybe the house of a Spanish-American or a wetback's house! The room I was looking into was about the size of our living room at home.

Then one of the most interesting things I ever saw in my life happened. A woman with sparkling jewels in her black hair lit another match, carried it over to the wall across the room and lit a candle, which was standing on a table. The flickering light from the candle lit up something that was hanging on the wall. It looked like a—like a— Say! It *was!*—a great big crucifix as big as a boy—a crucifix as you maybe know being a figure of the Saviour fixed to a cross.

Then I saw the woman drop down on her knees, look up to the crucifix for a while like she was talking to it with her mind.

While she was doing that the music outside stopped and everything was very quiet. A jiffy later the woman with the jewels in her hair turned, left the candle burning and came and stood in the doorway and called in a low, musical voice something in both Spanish and English and the English was: "You sing very beautifully, Pedro."

She came on out then and walked over to a bench beside the palm tree and the man with the guitar came out from behind the tree trunk and they sat down on the long bench together, one on one end and the other on the other, and the man began to play and sing again.

It looked like even though our adventure had come to life, the kind of life it had come to wasn't any of two boys' business, so I said to Poetry, "Let's get out of here."

"Yeah," he said, "let's," with a disgusted tone of voice. "That's probably a Mexican calling on his Mexican sweetheart,"—which Dad says is the way some Mexican senors do what is called "court" their senoritas—a senor being a man and a senorita being a lady of some age or other, who for some reason isn't married yet.

Pretty soon between the senor's verses we heard some different music coming from farther away and this time it was a lot of people singing a hymn.

80

Poetry and I started out as fast as we could go, both of us in the same direction, toward the new music, and we got back to the back of the tent just in time to see and hear the boy evangelist dismiss the service, also in time to stop at least two of our chaperons from starting to worry about us.

We had had a queer adventure, but I was disappointed because we had lost our twenty-five-cent boy. If only we could find out where he and his dad had gone—if he was his dad. I felt as bad as Mom does sometimes when she loses her glasses or her fountain pen and Dad and I have to stop doing whatever we are doing and help her look for it until she finds it again, right where she had thought it was in the first place.

But say! I needn't have felt so bad about our adventure being a flop because it certainly wasn't over yet. You see, when Poetry is with us, he being the kind of boy he is, whenever there is anything that even looks like it might have an adventure in it, he always wants to investigate and sometimes we run kersmack into one when there wouldn't have been any at all.

Anyway, as I said, I needn't have worried because we did see Dad's twenty-five-cent Mexican boy again and this time his back was really wet.

If I can, I will get going on that very exciting part of this story for you in the very next chapter of this book.

7

NEXT DAY we drove to Old Point Lighthouse at Port Isabel, but we couldn't get in because it had been closed for years and locked. We also went fishing off the jetties in Laguna Madre in the Gulf of Mexico near Padre Island. Some of the water in the Gulf of Mexico, a few drops of it anyway, used to be up in Sugar Creek, we decided, and we had probably gone swimming in it, but I guess the fish in the Gulf didn't know the difference, anyway they didn't bite at all. The wind was blowing so hard and the waves were so high and it was the lonesomest-looking place I was ever in in my life. Not a one of us even got a bite except Big Jim, who landed two anemic-looking catfish that weren't any longer than from his wrist to his elbow.

About all we got out of that day was a good launch ride, the name of the launch being "Gulf Pirate."

Our guide for the day was the boy evangelist's friendly father, who drove us all around the country in his station wagon. It was very interesting to discover that the boy evangelist was also a human being who enjoyed having fun as much as if he was an ordinary boy or a member of the Sugar Creek Gang. He and his dad had brought with them some gospel tracts, which are called color-tone tracts, and invitations to the tent meetings, which they distributed everywhere we went.

It was a good idea, we thought, so at Port Isabel the gang scattered itself all over the town, passing out color-tone tracts in all the stores to nearly everybody we saw.

"Where's that fish as big as a boy you were bragging about?" Poetry asked me that afternoon as he and I, side by side, went into and out of stores in a town called Mercedes, handing out tracts and invitations to the tent meetings.

"What fish as big as what boy?" I said, defending myself with an indifferent tone of voice.

Saying it, I thought how much more fun it would have been fishing with a dead bamboo pole and landing a six-inch-long chub out of the riffle just below our Sugar Creek swimming hole. At least a guy could get a *bite* in Sugar Creek anyhow. Before we went back to the hotel where our chaperons would be waiting for us to eat supper, we drove out to see a place called "The Cat," which was the absolutely most interesting and most sad-looking place I ever saw. "The Cat" was about forty houses made out of sticks and pieces of tin and palm branches and woven willows. The whole place was about as big as the three-acre plot below the pignut trees on our farm.

A dozen bashful-acting, half-dressed Mexican boys and girls stopped playing in their grassless yards and stared at us.

But I guess they must have known the boy evangelist and his dad 'cause the minute the father stepped out of the car with a handful of tracts rolled in red cellophane—making them look like a handful of stick candy—the children came running from every direction and we helped pass out maybe a hundred Spanish gospel tracts.

Driving on to the hotel, Poetry, who was seated beside me in the middle seat of the station wagon, said, "What's that song you're whistling, Bill?"

"What song?" I asked and pulled my thoughts back from "The Cat" where they had been and fastened them onto the tune that had been galloping around in my mind when I didn't even know it, and the song was "I Will Make You Fishers of Men." I was surprised to find out what it was, and for just a second I thought about what a funny thing a boy's mind is. He could be thinking about "The Cat" and riding in a station wagon and at the same time be whistling a song and not even know that he was whistling it.

* * *

Well, the days flew past too fast and, before we hardly realized it, there were only two days of our vacation left. Our chaperons had been having a wonderful time they said, just sitting around in the sun in their hotel patios, and the gang had been doing different things which boys like to do, even borrowing and reading some books from the public library, which was in a basement room under the bandstand in the park across from the hotel.

Our adventure would have to hurry up and come to life again, I thought, or we would have to go back to Sugar Creek without ever knowing how it would have ended. Not having any fish as big as a boy to talk about, it would be hard to take all the kidding which the people would give me. Dad, who had been reading the news, found out that the coal miners' strike was over so we didn't have any excuse for not going back home to the ten-below-zero weather they were having up there, and to the seventeen boy-battered desks in our one-room, red brick schoolhouse, which would have to have a roaring coal fire in the Poetry-shaped iron stove. The kids who sat up close to the stove would be smothering, and the ones in the back of the room would be able to see the frost in the air every time they exhaled.

We'd soon all be suffering our way through arithmetic and history and also geography. I knew that every time I would look at a map of the United States my eyes would drop down to the bottom of it to the Mexican border and I would wish summer would hurry up and come to Sugar

Creek. I decided that I liked summer in the summertime at Sugar Creek better than I liked summer in the winter on the Mexican border.

Poetry and I were seated on the glider in our upstairs, over-the-garage apartment porch when all of a sudden he, who had been reading the *Rio Grande Valley News*, gasped and said, "Hey, Bill, look, will you?"

First my eyes took in a wide circle all around our porch. I noticed that not a one of the rest of the gang was there. They were down on the lawn tossing a softball around and making a lot of boy noise.

Then I looked at the news heading Poetry's fat forefinger was pointing to and it said:

"WETBACK MIGRATION COSTLY IN LIVES AND MONEY"

Before my eyes had glanced halfway down the story I exclaimed, trying to be funny, "Oh, my aching wetback!"

"It isn't funny," he said. "Read all of it," which I did and even before my eyes had gotten to the last paragraph of the exciting story I wished I could have been a policeman or a detective and could have protected some of the Mexicans who had been killed by some very terribly wicked men.

"It's a shame to let all that excitement go on without our gang getting mixed up in it," Poetry said.

"I don't think it's fair myself. Hey!" I exclaimed. "What—?"

The softball Circus had just thrown to Little Jim down by the palm tree struck the top of Little Jim's glove, glanced off and up and struck the side of my head, which I had been resting against the screen. It startled me out of what few wits I had.

"Watch your step down there," I yelled down to the gang, and Circus called back, "That wasn't a *step*, that was a softball hitting a soft *head*," which I didn't think was very funny because I had just been reading about a wetback whose body had been found in the Rio Grande last night and his head had been bashed in by a murderer.

"Hey, you guys," Big Jim called up to Poetry and me. "The station wagon is stopping out in front. We're going on another drive!"

"Who wants to go on a dumb drive?" I called back.

What I really wanted to do was to find out where the wetback had been killed last night and go and see the place myself. As I said, it didn't seem right for there to be so much adventurous excitement going on so close by and the Sugar Creek Gang not having a chance to get into the middle of it—like I always try to do when a whirlwind starts moving across one of our fields back home; I always stop whatever I am doing and race out to it and try to run in the middle of it wherever it goes.

I told Poetry what I thought, but he answered, "It's too far—away up the Rio Grande near a little town called Roma. Besides you might get your own head bashed in."

"It might be safer than staying around *here*," I said, feeling the side of my head where the hard softball had struck it.

Our four chaperons had gone to Brownsville that day where two of them were going to do some exciting shopping in some exciting shops to get a lot of useless trinkets to stand on our mantels and window ledges at home—also they had promised a lot of other Sugar Creek mothers they'd bring back something for them. So the boy evangelist's father was taking care of us—even though not a one of us needed taking care of. He was going to drive us to a park of some kind where we would cook our own supper in Indian style on a sandy beach along the Rio Grande.

So far I had only seen the Rio Grande on a map and from a high bridge while we were crossing it. Of course, I had seen some of its brown water flowing through irrigation ditches, but today, our next to the last day in the valley, we were going to see it close up.

8

AFTER WE HAD LEFT the highway, we drove—
what seemed like miles and miles—over dusty,
narrow roads through the dusty brush, which I
later found out was made up of prickly pear cactus, bald cypress, horse chestnut, cottonwood poplar, ebony, burr oak, *huisache,* and what is called
honey mesquite. There were also a lot of fierce-
looking cacti called Spanish bayonet, but most of
the cacti were prickly pear cactus, which the In-
dians feed to their cattle after they have cut off
all the prickly parts.

After quite a long while we came to a little
clearing and there in front of our eyes was the
wide, muddy river bordered with different kinds
of willows, which I found out later were mostly

sandbar and black willow and also buttonbush willow. Some of the buttonbush willows were growing in the water close to the shore.

For a while Circus seemed kind of glum because even though there were plenty of trees they were all different from the kinds that grew at Sugar Creek. Hardly a one of us felt at home. In fact, I felt almost as bashful in that park with all those strange trees standing around staring at us as I do when we have company at our house. A lot of the trees had thorns on them, which meant we couldn't climb them or play games in them. Besides, they were too dusty. We would get our clothes all dirty if we did.

But we did have a lot of fun. We didn't expect to be left alone all to ourselves though, but the boy evangelist's father had to drive back to town to do some shopping, also to broadcast a special program advertising the tent meetings. He planned to be back in time to have supper with us and drive us all back to the tent.

Not a one of us thought about running into any danger because after all we were in what was called a public park. I say it was called that. If it had been a Sugar Creek park there would have been dozens and dozens of people around and cars and picnic baskets and a lot of kids yelling and playing and you wouldn't have to make your own excitement to be having a good time.

"I should be back around six o'clock for supper, but don't wait for me if I'm a little late. I'll be back in plenty of time to get you to the meeting tonight," the boy evangelist's father said. "You have everything you need, Big Jim?" he asked.

Our fuzzy-moustached leader nodded his head yes.

We did have everything we needed for a real Indian supper. There wouldn't be any danger of a brush-fire because we were going to build our fire on the beach itself where the only thing that could burn would be what we ourselves carried there. As you maybe know, we had had Indian suppers before, especially when we were on our camping trips in the summertime in the far north of the United States—but you maybe know all about that if you have read our exciting experiences in the book called *The Sugar Creek Gang Goes Camping*.

Right away we dug our eighteen-inch-square hole in the ground far enough up on the beach so there wouldn't be any Rio Grande water seeping into the bottom of it. We lined it with stones and then filled it with kindling wood and sticks. We piled other pieces of wood on top until the pile was about two feet high. Then Big Jim started the fire. We let it burn for a whole hour, feeding it with new, dry wood to keep a very hot fire all that time.

At the end of the fire's hour we scooped out all the ashes and live coals, leaving in the lining of terribly hot stones. Then we lined the whole hot hole with green leaves, mixing in a few lettuce leaves, which Big Jim had brought along on purpose.

As quick then as Mom could have done it herself, Big Jim laid in a big slice of steak apiece for each member of the gang and one for the boy evangelist's dad, also some potatoes and corn on the cob, which he had bought in a store, and carrots—which almost none of the gang liked but had to eat to keep our parents happy; besides carrots are supposed to be good for us, and maybe are.

On top of that we quick put more leaves, and piled more stones on top of the leaves, then we spread on a couple of soaking wet burlap sacks, enough to make a nice little mound like a small grave in a cemetery.

After about two hours our supper would be all cooked by the terribly hot steam from the hot rocks and the wet burlap sacks.

It was fun imagining ourselves to be pirates, who had sailed in from the Gulf of Mexico up the Rio Grande and buried our treasure there.

While we were waiting we played different games and told stories. We even played wetbacks and robbers, some of us pretending to be wetbacks and filling our pockets with small stones representing money, which we had earned in America picking grapefruit or pulling carrots and stuff. The rest of the gang would hide in the willows down by the river to waylay us. Somebody would yell, "OK, gang, it's dark now! It's time for the wetbacks to come out of the brush and get their backs wet swimming the river!" Only, of course, we didn't even get our *feet* wet. That river was such a big, wide, unfriendly thing that any boy would be silly to wade out into it. It certainly was different from Sugar Creek where we knew every inch of the bottom for a mile each side of the spring. We knew where every big rock was and every little riffle and every step-off. We even knew the names of some of the big bass that hid out in the deep water below the Sugar Creek bridge and nobody had caught them yet.

It gave me the creeps to even imagine myself taking even a few steps out into that big cold-hearted Rio Grande. Besides it certainly wouldn't be safe.

Well, time flew past too fast, yet hardly fast enough for me because I was hungry even before we buried our uncooked dinner in the ground.

"OK, wetback," Poetry said to me when he and I were alone close to the water's edge. He quick stooped, scooped up a handful of the Rio Grande and splashed some of it on my shoulders. "Let's go hide in the brush up there on that hill."

"Stop it," I exclaimed, swinging around and grabbing up a handful of water myself and making a "wet*face*" out of him.

But it was innocent fun and nobody let himself get mad, which is silly for a boy to do when he is playing any kind of a game.

"Look," all of a sudden Poetry said, "see that old black log over there across the river on the Mexican side?"

I looked across the unfriendly river to the gray and brown hills on the other side and sure enough there was a big black log. "What of it?" I said.

"It's too black for a log. You know what that looks like?"

"No, what?"

"It looks like an inflated rubber life raft. I'll bet somebody uses it for a boat. Somebody maybe gets paid for taking wetbacks back and forth so wetbacks won't get their backs wet."

I wished I had my binoculars, but of course I didn't have.

"Don't tell Dragonfly it's a rubber boat," Poetry said mischievously, "or he will be allergic to it and start sneezing."

Right that second from behind me Dragonfly did sneeze but it was because a little whirlwind of dust had come spiraling out of the brush and was heading across the beach toward the river.

"Hey!" I yelled all of a sudden at the whirlwind, starting toward it on the run. "Don't you *dare* cross that river," I yelled at it. "You can't carry all that dust across into Mexico without permission."

By the time I had said that, I was right in the center of the whirling dust and leaves and stuff which the whirlwind was stealing from Texas and was trying to take across into Mexico without paying duty on it.

Pretty soon it would be time to take our steak supper out of our hot-rock cooking utensil.

When six-thirty came and the station wagon still hadn't come, Big Jim said, "OK, gang, come and get it." It took only a few minutes to get the sand off the steaming burlap sacks, the top layer of stones off the leaves, and the leaves off the swellest, yummiest supper a boy ever cooked without a mother to worry about all the dirt he might accidentally eat.

After supper, when it began to get dark and still no station wagon came, we started to look at each other in our half-worried faces and to wonder how long we'd have to wait. It was about the lonesomest park I ever saw with not a single other human being having showed up all afternoon and not even the sound of a car.

The sun had already set and even though the afterglow was a very pretty pink and purple and gold, for some reason I didn't seem to enjoy it.

"Are there any wild animals down here?" Little Jim asked from within two inches of me where he sat crowded up close.

Not a one of us seemed to want to answer him because the answer would probably be yes and we didn't want to say out loud what our thoughts were already screaming at us in our minds.

In what seemed like only a jiffy it was dark; and it wasn't any nice, friendly dark either like it is up north along the creek. There weren't any bullfrogs bellowing bass solos in the riffles, or any big night herons crying, "Quok-quok!" as they fly up the bayou, or the splashing of a big bass feeding in the lily pads, nor the husky, rusty rustle of the blades of the corn. There wasn't even the rasping of palm tree leaves because this wasn't any civilized park, but one with only the native trees and bushes and the shrubs of Texas growing in it.

"We'd better get a fire started," Big Jim said, "so when he comes for us, or if he sends somebody else after us, they will see the light and know where we are."

We brought it to a vote as to whether to try to follow one of the many crisscrossing dusty roads back through the brush to the highway and thus run the risk of getting lost, or start a fire and stay by the river and wait, and the vote was six to nothing in favor of staying where we were.

It certainly wasn't a comfortable feeling all alone in the lonely dark. The river flowing through the buttonbush willows sounded like the hissing of a snake or something, and when we did hear sounds in the brush behind us, there wasn't a single sound I knew. It seemed like we were not only at the bottom of Texas but also at the very end of the world.

9

THE END of the world!

Of course, it wasn't that but when you are alone in a strange, wild country where gangsters hang out and it is night and your mind won't quit imagining all kinds of things that *might* happen, even when you've been wanting an exciting adventure, you wish whatever is going to happen will hurry up and do it, no matter how dangerous it is. You also half hope it *won't* happen.

I guess one reason I was worrying was because I figured my folks were doing it back at the hotel if they were home yet from Brownsville—or maybe by this time they were in the tent wondering why we weren't there too.

"Maybe Mr. Mulder had a flat tire," Big Jim

said casually, and I could tell he was trying to keep us calm by using a calm voice. "That rocky road leading into this wilderness is enough to give any tire a stone bruise or a blowout."

Big Jim decided to start the fire right away because, as he said, "If there *are* any wild animals around here, it will keep them away."

"*Wild animals!*" Dragonfly exclaimed in a frightened voice. "*Where?*"

"I said, '*If* there are,' " Big Jim answered. But his tone of voice still sounded like he was trying to keep the littlest one of us from being even more scared than we were. Then he yawned like he does when he is trying to be indifferent and started making a little wigwam of wood using that which we had left over from our afternoon fire.

Just then Dragonfly said, "Psst! Listen! I hear something coming!"

I was used to hearing him hiss like that up north when it generally didn't mean a thing—anyway nothing very important—although sometimes it did. But say! When he hissed like that right in the middle of our tense huddle, it made me feel nervous.

We strained our eyes and ears in different

directions. At first I didn't hear or see a thing. Then Circus said, "Look! It's somebody coming across the river."

I looked quick out across the shimmering waves of that wide Rio Grande expecting to see somebody wading or swimming across. But say! Actually, honest-to-goodness-for-sure, somebody *was* coming! I could see a long, black shadow right out in the moonlit middle of the river.

"It's our rubber life raft," Poetry said.

I guess we all saw it at about the same time. All the frightening things I had ever heard or read about wetbacks and labor trouble on the Mexican border—such as thirty-eight dead bodies being found in the river, the new wetback migration and the murder at Roma only yesterday—all these things came swarming into my mind like a half-dozen bumblebees at Sugar Creek when I accidentally poke a stick into their nest.

Big Jim quick stopped starting a fire.

To move from where we were or not to move, was the question. We could scramble up the bank into the brush and hide, but who wanted to get scratched up with cactus or mesquite or cat's claw, or run the risk of getting hurt by a wild animal or something? So we hid ourselves as well as we could behind the nearby buttonbush willows.

It seemed like we were all so scared we couldn't move, and, all the time, fast second after fast second, the black boat was coming nearer to our beach. I could already hear the splashing of paddles in the water.

"Anybody see how many there are in the boat?" Big Jim asked.

"Looks like only one," Dragonfly said, and it did.

" 'Smatter, you cold?" I asked Little Jim, who was shivering against my shivering arm. He didn't answer for a second, but he did press a little closer against me.

Then he astonished me by having a sense of humor right in the middle of that danger. He said, "I'm getting up close to you so you won't be s-scared!"

"If there's only *one* in the boat," Big Jim said, "then he isn't bringing any wetbacks over from Mexico. He's coming over here to take some back with him!"

Say, that sent a shower of scared shivers all over me as Big Jim added, "That means that somewhere behind us in the brush there is a wet-back or two or more hiding, waiting until the boat gets here, then they will dash down the bank, climb in and be rowed back."

"Look!" Poetry exclaimed, "he's rowing straight for *us!*"

I might have guessed he would. Of course, he would want the boat to be protected from sight by some growth along the shore, and the button willows we were hiding in would be just right.

Nearer and nearer the boat came and also—it seemed—faster and faster.

Then a flashlight went on and off three times in the boat. A second or two later from the bank up the shore, there was an answer—three fast, fleeting flashes.

Poetry, on the other side of me from Little Jim, whispered, "Anybody want to play a game of wetbacks and robbers now?"

"It's the wrong time to be funny," Circus said.

And Big Jim cut in with a calm, low voice, "There isn't anything to be afraid of. We are getting a good education without having to study. In a minute we will see acted out in real life the things we have been reading about—wetbacks being transported across the Rio Grande. In years to come we can tell about it to our children and our grandchildren."

Dragonfly interrupted him by saying, "If we live that long."

Say, when the boat came to within twenty-five feet of the shore, all of a sudden it stopped coming nearer and the lone man began paddling faster, going up along the shore and around a little neck of land at the end of our beach.

"Maybe he saw us," Big Jim said.

We all sat there, wondering what next, when all of another sudden, right in front of our eyes, the boat was empty and the river's current had caught it and whirled it about and it was floating back downstream with nobody in it. One minute the man had been in the boat and the next he wasn't.

We hadn't even seen him climb out—not even *fall* out. But say, instead of carrying the boat on past us downstream, it looked like the current was pushing it toward the beach again, which I decided it was, because the next thing I knew it had come to rest against the shore in a little cove not more than twenty-five yards from the button willows we were hiding in.

My eyes started chasing on up and down the river to see where on earth whoever it was had gone.

"You think he fell out and drowned?" whispered Little Jim.

Poetry whispered back, "He might have seen or heard us and thought we were officers and got scared and jumped out and swam to shore or maybe swam back toward the other shore—maybe swimming under the water."

"But nobody saw him in the water," I said. "He would have to come up for air sometime."

"Maybe somebody up there in the brush shot him with a gun that had a silencer on it," Poetry said, "and he just tumbled out."

It didn't seem possible that with our twelve eyes watching the boat not a one of us had seen what happened.

I turned the idea over in my mind. At the same time my mind itself seemed to be turning over and over.

Well, a gang of inquisitive boys couldn't be quiet too long or they would get the heebie-jeebies, so Poetry said, "Let's send out a couple of spies to the boat to see what happened"—which meant that he was still halfway between playing a game and real life. Then he added, "Maybe he *did* get shot and just fell into the bottom of the boat and that's why we can't see him."

Big Jim didn't like the idea of sending out spies. He said, "If somebody shot him, then the very minute any of us stepped out into that moonlight we'd probably get shot ourselves."

Only a second after that, things really started to happen. Quicker'n a flash, from up the bank there were running steps, and a man and a boy shot out into the moonlight, swished past our hiding place and on toward the boat.

"Our adventure again," Poetry hissed to me.

"Dad's twenty-five-cent boy," I said back to him.

Talk about brain-whirling excitement! I never was so close to that kind in my life without getting into the middle of it. Right away there were three people at the boat instead of two. The third one had risen up from behind the boat with a paddle in his hands. With a fast, fierce movement he raised the oar high and brought it down with a

110

smash on the head of the other man, who let out a wild yell of pain, threw up his arms, staggered backward and slumped down into the sand at the side of the boat, and also at the very edge of the water.

Before I could get my excited, muddled brain to thinking, Dad's twenty-five-cent boy and the third man were in a fierce, one-sided fight and I could hear grunts and socks and clothes tearing. I could also see the boy's fists flying faster than mine did that time I had my fierce fight up north with Shorty Long.

Any minute I expected the boy to get knocked flat, which he would if the man's fist ever hit him just right.

"Let's rush out and help him," Circus said, saying what most of us probably thought.

But Big Jim stopped us, saying firmly, "No, not yet. That might be an arresting officer employed by the Mexican or the American government, whose business it is to stop wetbacks."

Then something else began to happen. There was the sound of quick running steps sounding like a boy eating soda crackers very fast and I saw that little guy come rushing across the sand

111

toward our hideout. He got two-thirds of the way to us before the man caught up with him, grabbed him and slammed him on his back to the ground. A second later the man was on top of him holding him down and saying a lot of angry-sounding Spanish words at him!

Talk about anybody's temper getting ready to explode! Mine was like a lighted firecracker with a very short sputtering fuse. I wanted to see the boy get away because I was not only sure the savage man was a robber, but my sense of fair play made me want to see the man get the living daylights knocked out of him. I also had a lightning-flash mental picture of that little guy down on his knees in the tent giving his heart to God.

Along with my ready-to-explode temper there was also a warm love for that swell little guy. It wasn't any of my business whether he was a wetback or not, but it was my business to do something to help keep a human being from getting hurt by a big bully.

The man kept on yelling down into the boy's face some terribly fast Spanish words that sounded like he was swearing at him.

Well, if there is anything that makes me sadder in my heart than anything else, it's to hear a person take the Saviour's name or the heavenly Father's name in vain. I wondered quick what Little Jim was thinking. I knew swearing not only made him feel sad, but it also blew up his small temper till it was as big as a balloon at a county fair.

As you maybe know, Big Jim understood a little Spanish, so when he said to us, "He's swearing," it was too much for Little Jim—and that's how our whole gang got mixed up in the fight too. We had to get into it or let Little Jim get the living daylights knocked out of him. Almost the very second Big Jim told us the man was swearing, Little Jim was gone from beside me and I saw a streak of moonlit, curly-haired boy shooting out from the shade of our willows across the sand and making a flying-tiger leap straight for the back of the neck of the bully. He got there only about five seconds before five other boys did.

Talk about a scramble. That was really one. Our battle with that fierce-fighting wild man was something. I say *wild* because when six boys landed on him from about six different directions at the same time, he started acting like a man that had suddenly gone crazy, like a chicken that has just had its head cut off.

I didn't know much of anything for a while—like a boy doesn't when he is excited or mad and in a fight—but I did sort of realize three things: one was that our robber wasn't an American because he was swearing in Spanish; also he was all wet, which meant he had slipped out of the boat when it was still in the river and had swum or waded along behind it pushing it to the shore, making it look like there wasn't anybody in it at all; and he was as strong as an ox.

If we hadn't been a husky gang of boys, we would have all been hurt pretty bad. For a half second I even thought I was glad my parents had made me hoe potatoes and do all kinds of other hard farm work because when I got my arm around that bird's wet hind leg with sand on it, I shut my eyes and gritted my teeth and held on like a bulldog. Circus had a hold on his other leg; and Big Jim, Poetry, Little Jim and Dragonfly were doing other things to the rest of him. Also the minute he could, Dad's twenty-five-cent boy scrambled to his feet and helped us hold the man down.

"Get me one of the gunnysacks, Bill," Big Jim ordered me.

"Why?" I asked.

Already Big Jim was feeling fine and he said mischievously, "To put our fish in. Didn't you say you were going to catch a fish as big as a boy? Well, here's one as big as a man."

I was back in a jiffy with the gunnysack.

"Now," Big Jim said, panting and holding onto the man's arm, "get the fishing line out of my hip pocket."

In only a minute or two we had the man's feet shoved into the gunnysack and Big Jim's fishing line wrapped round and round his ankles.

Almost the very second we finished tying him up, a car swung up to the shore above us and a spotlight lit up the whole beach where we were.

And then the most astonishing thing happened. The light hadn't any sooner focused on our tangled-up scramble than our little Mexican boy took one frightened eye-blinking look at it, jumped like a scared rabbit, whirled around and started on a wild dash for the river, where he plunged in

115

and splashed his way out through the shallow water until it was too deep for him to wade any farther. Then he began a fierce, fast swim toward Mexico.

10

CRAZY THINGS were really going on on the Mexican border that night. The story the Sugar Creek Gang could tell to their grandchildren was going to be very exciting as well as very interesting. The only thing was it ought not to be too long. If we told it to our grandchildren at night as a bedtime story, they wouldn't want us to stop in the middle but would cry for more, and if we kept on till we got to the end, it'd be too late for the littlest ones to stay up.

I could very easily imagine myself being a grandfather with a couple of wriggling, squirming grandchildren on my lap—with maybe one of them using my long, thick reddish whiskers for a pillow.

117

Well, there we were—six panting boys holding a wild man down on his stomach, on a sandy beach along the Rio Grande. A bright spotlight from somebody's car was shining on us. Another man with a hurt head was lying up the beach twenty-five yards from us, and the Mexican boy we had tried to rescue was swimming like mad toward his native land—crossing the Rio Grande alone.

That is, I thought he was going to have to cross it alone. For a second the spotlight swung away from us and I noticed it was focused on the swimming boy out in the river.

"Hey!" Poetry, whose eyes were looking where mine were, exclaimed. "There's another boat out there! He's climbing into it!"

My half light-blinded eyes looked quick toward the place where the first boat had been, but it wasn't there.

Also gone was the man who ten or more minutes before had gotten his head socked with a boat paddle and had been lying beside the boat. That could mean only one thing, and that was that the boy's dad—if he was his dad—had regained his consciousness—if he had lost it—and still had strength enough to paddle the boat.

By the time my eyes could get back to the twenty-five-cent boy again he was already in the boat and was helping paddle back to the other side.

All this time our prisoner was struggling fiercely and we were still holding on for dear life. We knew we didn't dare let loose for a second 'cause if he had a knife like some Mexican criminals do have, he'd probably use it on us.

Right away, two men who had been in the car which had the spotlight were hurrying down the bank to our battlefield to take our prisoner off our hands.

In a jiffy the officers—which is what they were—were taking charge and doing different things which arresting officers do, such as putting handcuffs on our prisoner and asking us a lot of questions and stuff.

They had us tell the whole story which we did, using six different excited voices to do it. It turned out that we had caught one of the worst criminals Mexico had ever had. He had broken out of a Mexican jail named the Black Palace, at Mexico

City. Both the United States government and the Mexican government had been looking for him. The only thing was, as soon as he gave up he didn't act like a vicious criminal. In fact, he didn't even look like one. He had a haircut and shave and he answered questions in a polite voice. Also, he could talk English almost as well as Spanish.

"It's a wonder one of you boys didn't get slashed to pieces," the tallest officer said to us.

"Which one?" Dragonfly asked.

The shorter officer, whose face I could see pretty well in the moonlight, grinned and said to Dragonfly, "You, probably." Then he added, talking to our prisoner, "Well, Pedro, let's get started. You're going back to live in the palace again. They've been missing your singing down there."

Pedro! Singing! Poetry and I gasped at each other at the same time, and my imagination picked me up and carried me over the top of the dusty brush—the mesquite and cottonwood poplar and bald cypress and prickly pear cactus—to a grapefruit grove and a weather-scarred tin-roofed house, and I was seeing a black-haired senorita lighting a candle before a boy-sized crucifix, and a man with a guitar singing behind a palm tree. Boy,

120

oh boy! Poetry and I had been a whole lot closer to a live adventure that night than we realized. Pedro had probably been following the twenty-five-cent boy and his dad that very night, trying to find out when they were going back to Mexico.

In the excitement of things, I had almost forgotten about the boy and his dad—if it was his dad. I had even forgotten my own dad and our other three chaperons—also the boy evangelist's dad, who still hadn't come for us.

But a little later while we were still on the beach the station wagon came swinging down one of the park's dusty roads to where we were. All three dads were in it—the boy evangelist's, Dragonfly's and mine.

It took only a little while for them to explain why anybody hadn't come sooner. The police had set up what is called a "roadblock" at the park entrance, and no cars except police cars had been allowed to enter.

"It's this way," one of the officers explained. "We discovered that wetbacks were using rubber life rafts from Army surplus stores. A wetback would row across the river, tie the boat to shore and leave it for some other wetback to use for a return trip. Pedro, just out of jail, found out about it and was cashing in on it, and—you know the rest of what happened. Thanks to you boys, he tried it once too often."

Well, this has got to be the last part of this story, because nothing else happened that was very important until we got back home to Sugar Creek.

In the station wagon on the way to town, Dragonfly, who was sitting beside me in the middle seat, sneezed three times in fast succession—the first time I'd heard him sneeze that many times that fast for an hour or two.

"Hey," I said to him, "don't start that again! You haven't sneezed for over an hour. How come?"

Dragonfly giggled and said, "I guess I forgot. I can sneeze anytime I want to, though!"

"You cannot," Poetry challenged him.

"I can too," Dragonfly argued back.

"All right then, let's hear you do it."

Dragonfly answered in a saucy voice, saying, "I'm sorry, but I don't happen to want to"— which was an old joke and was maybe a little bit funny.

Well, we had a wonderful vacation, and especially a wonderful next-to-the-last day, but I wasn't satisfied. It seemed like most every minute of the way to town my mind's eye was seeing the little Mexican boy swimming like fury out to a rubber boat, climbing in and helping the man paddle as fast as they could, out across the moonlit Rio Grande to their own country. I didn't like the idea of having him swim out of my life like that 'cause I might never get to see him again. He would probably never get to become a citizen of the United States. If he did get to live over here, he'd have to be a wetback.

Little Jim helped me feel better about it when he said, "Maybe if he and his dad were really saved in the tent that night, they'll hunt up a preacher in Mexico who knows how to be saved in the way the Bible says and they'll join his church."

I could tell by the tone of voice Little Jim was using that he was getting sleepy. He rested his head against my shoulder, sighed a heavy sigh, and kept still, which made me feel pretty fine, 'cause if there's anything a boy likes, it is to have a boy he likes like him back.

I felt fine for another reason, which was that

after another day we would be leaving Texas and would be on our way back to Sugar Creek.

We hadn't caught any fish as big as a boy, but we had caught a fierce criminal, and by doing that had maybe helped keep a lot of wetbacks from getting killed.

I was surprised when Poetry said, from beside me, "What's that song you're whistling, Bill?"

"What song?" I asked, and listened to my thoughts. I was whistling the song "I Won't Have to Cross Jordan Alone."

It was a good song and I knew I would never forget it as long as I lived, and because I was a Christian I would probably remember it *after* I got through living. I might even sing it on my way to heaven.

During the week we had been in the Rio Grande Valley, we had heard the quartet sing it nearly every night. So, a jiffy later, when somebody in the station wagon started to sing it, the rest of us started in to help him.

Maybe some of us sounded a little bit like some of Mom's hens singing in our barnyard. Poetry's changing voice actually did sound like the snoring croak of a middle-sized bullfrog and mine didn't sound like anything. Only Circus' was good, which it always is—maybe because he vocalizes more than the rest of us. Sometimes he does it from the top branches of the elm sapling that grows along the bayou right where the old rail fence starts its lazy climb up Strawberry Hill, on top of which is the abandoned cemetery, where Old Man Paddler's wife is buried, and where—

Say! Did I ever tell you about the time the gang was coming home one dark night from fishing for catfish just above the Sugar Creek bridge, and on the way home decided to pass close to the cemetery to convince ourselves we weren't afraid to—and just as we got there we saw a lantern and somebody digging a hole behind a thicket of chokecherry shrubs!

I can't seem to remember telling you about that. So maybe my next story will be all about that mysterious adventure and the very strange acting person who was digging there—and why.